Pacifier
By Ira Rat

filthyloot.com

Pacifier
Copyright © 2018/2021 by Ira Rat
Book & cover design by Ira Rat

This is a work of fiction. Names, characters, businesses, places, events, locales, and incidents are either the products of the author's imagination or used in a fictitious manner. Any resemblance to actual persons, living or dead, or actual events is purely coincidental

This book may not be reproduced in whole or in part, except for the inclusion of brief quotations in a review, without permission in writing from the author or publisher. No part of this publication may be reproduced, stored in or introduced into retrieval system, or transmitted, in any form, or by any means (electronic, mechanical, photocopying, recording, or otherwise), without prior permission of the publisher.

Requests for permission should be directed to filthylootpress@gmail.com

SECOND EDITION

"Not a wasted word."

– Danger Slater (author, *I Will Rot Without You*, and *Puppet Skin*)

"Worshipers of Porcine Gods, sad days spent with agency-assigned strangers, and the healing properties of blood. In *Pacifier*, Ira Rat proves himself a master of crafting tightly-written, strange stories that are never at odds between beauty and darkness, the grotesque and emotional truth, but instead seamlessly do all in one fluid motion."

– Sam Richard (author, *Sabbath of the Fox-Devils*, and *To Wallow in Ash & Other Sorrows*)

"Ira is cynical without lacking sympathy, experimental without lacking direction. A dark, ambitious new voice."

– Garret Cook (author, *Archelon Ranch* and *A God of Hungry Walls*)

"The Stories in Ira Rat's *Pacifier* take subtle delight in exposing the reader to their twisted imagery and ethos. A treat for those of us with a taste for the darkly askew."

– Amy Vaughn (author, *Freak Night at the Slee-Z Motel*, and *Skull Nuggets*)

"Ira Rat's little collection, *Pacifier* provides four bite-sized morsels which are delightfully disturbing. There is a beauty to his quiet horror, creeping up in a strange and unsettling manner."

– S.T. Cartledge (author, *Beautiful Madness* and *The Orphanarium*)

"With stories that range from quiet sadness to barking insanity, Pacifier is a book that stays with you long after you've read it."

- Jon Steffens (author, *The God in the Hills*)

Also By The Author
Participation Trophy (Filthy Loot, 2020)
Hairs (Filthy Loot, 2023)
Endless Now (Filthy Loot, 2024)

THANK YOU TO EMILY, FOR EVERYTHING, ALWAYS.

I want to thank Cody Goodfellow, Garret Cook, Danger Slater, Sam Richard, Melanie Bowling, Amy M. Vaughn, Jon Steffens, Casey Jones, NIHILISMREVISED & everyone else who had eyes on this before it went to print or bought the first edition.

Last Good Day, Before Goodbye
9

Pacifier
28

Feedlot
52

The Butterfly of Ugly
78

Last Good Day, Before Goodbye

My fucking feet hurt, and I want to quit. We've been walking for the past couple of hours and I'm over it. I know that today is supposed to be a nice gesture, something to put me at ease, but it's more awkward than when I had agreed to it.

I should be grateful, I know. After all, she was the willing to do this for me. "Wherever you want to go," she said at the beginning of the day, trying to muster up as much enthusiasm she could. Clearly, she was just going through the motions for my sake, but could you blame her? It was just one last good day before goodbye.

We had already gone through a couple museums that were within walking distance. Unfortunately, most of the exhibitions have been pretty mediocre. I've often wondered how many people could have painted the Madonna with an anatomically-incorrect baby Jesus and, without fail, there was always a dozen more in all their glory.

For a while, I had become obsessed with depictions of St. Sebastian, though, after seeing a score of those, I began to realize that there were only so many places that the artist could think to put the arrows.

I picture myself with my arms held outstretched behind my back as a volley of arrows pierce my body. The crowd that had gathered looks on in bemused detachment. *Ooooh look hon, another martyr! This must be our lucky day. I thought for sure that there wouldn't be anything a'tall to watch!*

I just stand there and watch them watch me as I bleed out, keeping the pose like I was waiting for someone to whip out a palette and canvas to capture the moment in all its gory glory. Nobody cares; I wait for nothing until everything goes black. Surrounded by a pool of my own making. Martyred without the recognition of being one. I guess that's how it should be. The ones that were remembered must have been show offs.

Back in reality, I'm still here looking at what's playing at the art house theater we had come upon. Most of the movies look like low-budget potential token Oscar noms. I read the little capsule reviews on Xeroxed rocket red cardstock. "Shit, shit, shit, seen it, hate her. *Oh shit*, no way!" I say as my eyes finally find that they're playing _____. God, I hadn't seen that in forever, and never on the big screen.

This might actually be my lucky day, but probably not.

She nods in agreement as I tell her there is, in fact, a movie that I want to see playing. Her lack of enthusiasm doesn't put a stop to mine. Had she seen it? *Oh fuck, you haven't?* She buys the tickets, and we escape the August heat into the cool, gentle, air-conditioned purr of the movie theater. *I swear you'll love this.*

We sit and watch the movie, my feet growing less achy as the movie rolls on. As with all movies that you love, it's over too fast. So, in a blink, we're back out walking the street, and my feet pick up their complaints where they left off. "God, that gets better every time I see it. What did you think?" I ask, knowing full well from the look on her face she wasn't terribly impressed.

She shrugs, and we come to an impasse of what to do next.

I think to ask her what she wants to do, but she doesn't have any suggestions. After all it was *my day*. If she were the one to pick what we did, it would be *hers* and if it was *hers* she definitely wouldn't be walking around the city doing the stupid shit that I like to do. If it were *her* day, she wouldn't even be with *me*. It kind of goes without saying, you know?

I do have to say, she's being an awfully good sport about it. She owes me less than nothing.

She doesn't notice, but sometimes I see her looking at me with a sad little smile on her lips, as if she were getting some kind of enjoyment out of watching me do the things that I enjoy. That is kind of hard to ignore, honestly. Or maybe I'm just projecting.

I picture me and her on a beach somewhere. Maybe that's what she would prefer to be doing. We would watch the tide roll in as the sun started to set in some tropical locale that I wouldn't even begin to know the name of because I don't know places like that. I've never been out of the city; the city was my home. It was where I was born and, if all goes well, I'll die here too.

A few heads in front of us, I see a couple kiss, holding hands as they walk. I get the sudden urge to hold her hand. Fat chance of that, though. That was the first thing that she had told me before we even started this little trip around; *nothing affectionate, that's not what this is about.*

Okay. I had said. Okay.

My hand had started to gravitate towards hers subconsciously, but I jerked it back and put it into my pocket. Even if she were to show a little mercy and had held it, that's all it would have been. Mild comfort, not a genuine desire to connect. I could have been anyone to her.

What's the point of affection, if it means nothing?

She asks where I want to eat. Again, it's my day after all, I should pick. As with every time I've ever been asked this question, nothing really sounds all that fantastic. We're surrounded by a couple dozen restaurants within a few blocks and none of them scream, *eat me!*

I shrug and say that we should just go to the next place that we come across, which is an Indian restaurant. I could have chosen much worse if I had sat there contemplating it. This would do, considering. We both order curries with different kind of meat but decide to split an order of aloo tikki. The smells of the restaurant are alien from the distance of memory, but quickly become familiar to me.

The food is hot and good. The conversation is kind of cold, and not that great.

I ask her how her work is, she says that her editor has been on her ass for a week to get the next draft of her novel done.

"Oh, yeah?" I said. "I can't wait to read it!" I said without a trace of irony. Though this makes her frown. Do you ever have those moments in your life where you wish that you could read somebody's mind? She makes me want to so I can figure out this whole situation.

Out of all the comic book superpowers, reading minds had to be the one that would help out in just about every social situation. Especially for guys like me; I tend to not see all the social queues. *Would she have held my hand?* It's not like I would have another chance after tonight.

Women — can't read their mind, can't ask them what they're thinking. You learn the second part the hard way.

"Whatchu want to do next?" She asked, though I could see from her expression that she was tired, and probably had enough of placating me even though it had been her idea. After all, I had not asked her for any of this. Though considering how much she had put up with, I'm sure it was time to let her go on with her life.

"We can go back." I said with a little sigh. *It's time to rip the band-aid off, no?*

Pacifier

The room was cold, a little too cold to be comfortable, even though we had spent the day walking around in the heat. The dampness chilled me to the bone. Looking at her out of the corner of my eye, I could see that she seems a little upset. I wished there was something that I could do to comfort her, but considering everything, I'm not sure that would be appropriate for me to do.

"So how was your day out?" The man with the clipboard asked us. She shrugged and looked down, not being able to make eye contact with either of us.

I slowly shake my head yes, like, *it was good as it could be.* Though it would be inappropriate to respond with much of anything, considering the circumstance.

"Fantastic!" He said with all the fake enthusiasm of a well-paid maître d'. "Sign here." He held the clipboard out for me and I signed. The cheap Bic leaving a smear of ink as I sign my name.

"State law requires me to remind you that this procedure — while being a benefit for the overall well-being of the city — is completely *voluntary*." He added with the kind of weight that only comes with practice.

I shake my head, *yes, I know.*

"Fantastic! Alright while the nurse is getting ready, I just wanted to personally thank you for your service." He said before eye fucking my chaperone right in front of me.

"On a personal note, I think you're a hero." He

continued on with his pre-written routine. "You're *all* heroes, I mean!" He nodded his head behind him to a pile of bodies, there must be 50 or 60 of them.

Six or so deep.

The bottom ones had started oozing from the weight.

I wonder how often they actually clean out this room.

"After all, you're just the first wave. We'll all be along eventually." The fake modesty in his voice made me cringe.

Yeah, I know everyone will one day be where I'm going, I thought to myself a little bitterly. It had been my choice to make, but the smugness almost made me want to tell him to go fuck himself, grab my chaperone's hand, and run out the door.

Would she have come with me? It's not like we even knew each other. Hell, one of the rules is that I don't even know *her name*. Had I fallen for her in just a couple short hours walking around the city? Or was this just cold feet?

Too late to turn back now, I thought to myself, even though it wasn't going to.

The nurse came in wearing a candy striper outfit from a different era. A bit of theatrics, I thought, as she brought out the big silver tray with the needle on it. Did they have to make euthanasia any more dramatic? I was volunteering, after all.

I wonder what kind of focus group had

approved this.

Mr. Maître D' points me to a chair. *Here you go!* His motion tells me, and I do what I'm told.

The nurse comes over and opens the one-time use alcohol swab before applying it to the inside of my elbow. *Is this completely necessary?* I think to myself. *It's not like I'm going to get an infection after I'm dead.*

Better safe than sorry, I'm sure they would say.

I wonder how much money the city would save if they didn't do these swabs, or if they just used one of those bolt guns they use on cattle?

I'm sure that was deemed *inhumane. Whatever that means*, I think to myself. Whatever, beggars can't be choosers. What was inhumane was living in this city without prospects, without a future, without a woman – like *whatever her name is* – on your arm.

The nurse pokes me with the needle and sends the chemicals into my veins. It feels like a warm glow spreading throughout my body. I feel the sunshine on my skin as she and I stand on the beach. She kisses me, and we lock eyes, and everything is right with the world. Everything is beautiful.

"Alright, some housekeeping here." The man with the clipboard said, snapping me back into the room. "State law prohibits us from actually *moving you* after you... after it's done." He looks a little bashful, but you can tell that he's had to say this to hundreds, if not thousands, of people before. "They don't want the union breathing down their neck if we hurt our backs, so I'm *unfortunately* going to have to ask you to climb onto the top of the pile."

I stand dazed, not believing what I'm hearing, but then I hear the magic word.

"Please, if you don't mind."

I slowly start walking towards the mountain of dead flesh and put my hand down into the first available crevasse, which just happens to be s 40-year old woman's mouth, her Lennon glasses reflect my ghost as I look down. I stick my fingers in and start pulling up my weight. Her jaw comes down, and it hurts, but isn't enough force to break the skin. Next, I grab onto somebody's hip, and up I go. King of the mountain.

From down below, I hear him saying "Thanks," before turning to her.

"So, are you going to be volunteering next week? Same time as always?" He says, obviously hitting on her, even though I'm still right here. I'm still alive. She was my date for the day.

That's when I jump down from my perch and punch him right in his smug face. I'm the one person that this stuff doesn't work on! I've lived through death! Then I tell her that I don't know her, but I'm totally in love with her, and we should run off together. Maybe to our beach? She doesn't know what I'm talking about, but that's okay, because she's in love with me, too. It was love at first sight.

But I don't; I just sit there as the drugs begin

to take hold and the world begins to dissolve a little around the edges. From the top of the heap I answer for her, "She needs next week off, she's working on her novel."

Pacifier

Frank Herbing looked like someone out of one of those camps from those World War II films they made you watch in grade school, Dr. Adelman thought. If he had seen a five-digit number crudely tattooed on the boy's forearm, at least that would have explained why he looked so wasted away. Adelman had seen his fair share of tweakers, junkies, anorexics and bulimics over the years, but none of them had given him the impression of staring death right in the face until he first saw Frank sitting across from him that first day, nearly a year ago.

The kid was atrophied from undernourishment, his lips pulled back from his teeth in a grotesque parody of a smile. Shards of acid-etched enamel protruded from his gum line in a few places where the tooth had broken away. This kid took the prize even from some of the worst meth addicts that came in here.

He could see the kid dying right in from of him, but the thing is, he wasn't. It had been a year and all the tests came back the same. The thing that bugged Adelman more, was that the boy really wasn't living either. A boy his age should be out getting his wick wet, not sitting here in a free clinic, looking like an Auschwitz survivor.

The doctor's detached dark sensibility got

hammered into him in med school. *Smile for the patients, but never let them effect you.* It was an idea he had thought of as barbaric when he first started, because he felt that he cared about people. After his first patient had taken their life, it became his only mechanism to keep going. *Never let them in.* A philosophy his ex-wives could attest that he took to heart.

The simple fact was that he had cared too much even with this philosophy. So, when he saw Frank's name on the schedule, the bottle of Xanax in his pocket made sure he was good and numb.

If they lived in a more progressive state, maybe he would have the resources to find a solution for Frank. But as far as the current government was concerned, Hippocrates could go fuck himself and shove his oath somewhere dark and moist. Sometimes being dead *had* to be the better option. Coming back every month to visit a dime store doctor *and* de facto nutritionist with no answers wasn't any way to live. Especially when there wasn't any sign that he was getting any better. Or worse.

It had been a year, so what kept this kid going?

Adelman had tried to examine him the first time he came in, but he started screaming so much that Adelman was scared that Frank would have a heart attack. A full battery of tests was beyond the budget of the clinic, so he simply had him prick his own finger and sent what little urine he could get him to squeeze out to the lab. From what little results they got, he was stable.

Grasping at straws by the end of their last

appointment last week, the doctor prescribed and even sprang for high protein shakes, but he couldn't even keep *that* down. From what Frank told him, it just came right back up. As far as he could remember, it had always been that way, no matter what he ate.

What could he do, if Frank couldn't even keep a *shake* down?

As far as Adelman could tell, Frank was likely to die any day now, yet he'd been staring down that same prognosis since his first visit. The question of how he had survived this long was a medical anomaly far above his pay grade. This was hardly John Hopkins and being the most respected doctor in a storefront clinic didn't exactly amount to much.

As always, Frank walked home alone, not even bothering to look before walking through traffic. Nobody ever hit him, just slammed on their brakes and stared at him like they just got a free ticket to a freak show. How could he blame them? If he saw someone who looked like him, he would gawk, too.

Often, his only contact with the outside world was the Samaritan who came by twice a week to deliver generic cans with white labels reading "beans" or "vegetables," or sometimes just "meat." They used to bring him higher-end generic food like you found in real stores, with names like "Pasta Rings," but once word about his condition got back to the food bank, they decided to save those for someone who could keep them down.

His room was spare and clean, but still

somehow reeked from all the sick that had been spilled. He stayed in this shithole building because nobody else lived on the floor. Whether it was that other potential tenants had seen him or had heard the woman downstairs who sounded like she was dying of tuberculosis, a sound you could plainly hear from anywhere in the building, he didn't know.

He just knew that the lack of other bodies was mildly comforting.

Sometimes, he hoped that she could somehow give him her disease through the floorboards. If he could just catch something terminal, maybe he wouldn't have to continue to endure. The pain wasn't just in his stomach; maybe if it were, he could handle that. His whole body ached so insidiously that the fires of hell would be a welcome relief.

Haunted by thoughts that he would be in this suspended agony for another sixty years was the thing that scared Frank the most. He had gone a week without eating once, and not even that had *done the trick*. So, he jumped back into the cycle. He didn't *not* want to. His body just rejected anything he attempted to put in it.

From his window, he watched and imagined picking fights with people on the street. Who would be most capable of killing him? Hipster Jesus, or the bodybuilder walking the chihuahua? It didn't really matter, as long as they did it *quickly*. The thought of them failing, of him lingering on after someone had *touched* him was something that made his skin crawl. The thought of human contact repulsed him worse than anything else he could think of. Worse than the pain that filled his waking hours.

Not even his doctors had been allowed such intimacy.

He knew it was a ridiculous thought. There were about a million ways that he could take his own life, and he had entertained them all. However, every time he Googled the options on his phone, he would see stories of people who lived through every one of them. The thought of surviving an attempt seemed so much worse. Killing himself was out of the question; willingly putting himself in harm's way seemed the better option.

Looking in a mirror left in the apartment by the previous tenant, Frank watched himself suck his thumb. He looked like a baby in a hunger relief ad. He'd cut it opening a can of "meat" that might have been beef or tuna, he couldn't tell which. Didn't really matter, anyway. Once it got past his river-stone-smooth molars, it was back up again in a few seconds. He didn't even notice how badly he was bleeding until he went to wash his hands, but decided not to.

Ugh, so much blood, he thought as he watched the crimson stream slowly turn into a gel on his thumb. He had the sudden urge to stick it in his mouth.

The memory of boy-smell filled his nose, making him bristle with unease. *Oooooh, look at the little baby*, the voices in his head mocked as they threw stones at him. He had broken the habit when he was six. The older kids at the orphanage had seen it as an open invitation to fuck with him. *I'll give you something to suck on!* When the lights went out, they often did just that. *Come on baby, suck the pacifier.*

However, the sensation of his thumb in his mouth comforted him. The coppery taste of his blood almost put him at ease. Come to think of it, sitting here alone in his room while sucking his thumb—this was the best he felt in years.

Maybe ever.

For the next several days, his tongue wiped

the corners of the wound to keep it open. Purple and prune-like, his thumb was rarely a few inches away from his suckling lips.

His stomach rumbled, and a sensation he hadn't felt in months filled his bowels. Adelman had pointed out early on that he'd known opioid addicts with more regular bowel movements than him. He excused himself from his chair by the window and went into the chilly white-tiled tomb of his bathroom.

So much blood.

It looked like an animal had gotten trapped under a lawnmower. Flushing the evidence of his evacuation, he realized his bladder was also quite full. He reluctantly unzipped his blood-speckled jeans and pulled out his *thing*, an organ he didn't like to think about. It often felt gross, even to know it was hiding down there in that jungle of hair.

The red arc looked dazzling, glistening in the fluorescent light.

Dr. Adelman looked at Frank in his office, explaining what was going on. If it wasn't for the man's milky anemic complexion, he would have had a hard time believing that Frank had digested enough blood to pass the way he described. The one thing his year with Frank had done was expand his perception of what the human body could endure.

He'd asked Frank often if he suffered suicidal intentions. In so many words, Frank always responded by rambling about the difference between the desire for death and taking your own life in a post-god world. Frank and Camus might have made a great coffee klatch, the doctor thought.

In the end, he cleaned the cut and poured an obscene amount of Vetbond into the wound, squeezing it into a smarmy little smile on his thumb. He applied a bandage to it and nylon mesh pressure wrap over that, while giving Frank a halfhearted lecture about how self-harm wasn't a laughing matter. It was the same lecture he gave the cutters and wrist-bangers, knowing full well that they were just going to go home and do it again.

His heart went out to Frank. Well, as much as his heart would go out to anyone. His heart belonged to Pfizer.

Frank sat at his window, resisting the urge to rip off his bandages and suck his thumb. He wondered if he could take hipster Jesus one on one, drag him up to his room, and feed off him for the next few days. Maybe he could do it like that serial killer he'd once read about: lure victims up to his apartment with the promise of sexual favors. No, he wouldn't be alluring to anyone, not the way he looked.

Maybe if he was able to get a few meals down, he wouldn't look like Tom Hanks in *Philadelphia*. Though if he was able to get anything to stay down, he wouldn't even have to contemplate any of this.

Even if he could get them up here, what would he kill him with? He had no muscles to speak of, and poison didn't sound like the wisest move, with what he wanted to do with them. He imagined finding a heroin addict, hopefully weaker than him, and latching onto their track marks like a leach in the back of an alley way.

The thought having to touch someone, as always, made him tremble. Tears stung his eyes. *Come on baby, suck the pacifier.* The dozens of voices inside his head repeated, overlapping each other in a cacophonous choir.

Frank's bowels rumbled. Twice in one week—that might be a personal record!

Standing before the commode, he couldn't bring himself to flush, having noticed that it almost looked like fresh blood, but it had a slaughterhouse floor coagulated quality that turned him away.

Moving to the sink to wash his hands, he never took his eyes off the toilet. He dried his hands and put the towel back on the metal hoop, dropping to his knees in front of the porcelain.

The thought of reaching in and scooping out the contents into his mouth made him gag.

He couldn't, but he had an idea.

He hurried to the kitchen, grabbing a dusty drinking glass from the cupboard and brought it back to the bathroom. He filled it with a fine red stream, before downing it in one gulp.

The blood in his stomach just came right back out with a tremendous splash.

It was too much, the tears from earlier became a flood. The voice in his head taunted him. *Suck it, baby. Yeah suck it.*

He ripped off the bandages from his thumb, and ripped open the wound with his teeth, loosening a canine in the process. On the morgue-cold floor, he wept and suckled.

Frank's dead. Adelman thought after he had missed several appointments. He pictured him dead and rotting away in some nondescript apartment. It had been nearly four months, and he couldn't shake the dull melancholy that nobody would find him until rent was passed due. Nobody deserved that.

Frank's address was in his file, but even after Adelman noticed that it was just down the street, it took him several days to get up the nerve to go. He should call the police, but if he did and Frank was just fine, he would look crazy.

Finally, the day came that he couldn't shake the feeling that if he didn't find the boy, nobody would for a long time. Even if they did, how would he know? He had been scanning the papers for an obituary, though if the kid didn't have a family, would there even be one?

He took an extra Xanax before leaving work. The street was hot, even for 8 o'clock, as they were staring down fall.

When he got to the building, he was surprised that it looked abandoned. In this neighborhood full of people looking for cheap rent, people seemed to be actively avoiding it.

The stairwell was clean, but dusty. He could hear a woman coughing as he passed the third floor. Frank's was on the fourth, at least by his apartment number.

To his surprise, Frank answered the door. Even more alarming was that Frank looked healthy. His lips nearly covering his grotesque smile. He looked almost human for the first time.

At first, he couldn't find words, though Frank looked at him expectantly.

"I just came to see how you were doing." The doctor said, when his eyes were drawn to the boy's hands. The fingertips appeared to have been chewed on by rats, looking into the apartment he could see little trails of blood on everything that Frank had touched.

There was no scabbing, at least none that he could see from this distance. Just the raw, pinkish meat that peeked from the ragged edges of his fingernails.

"Come in." Frank said with a little hesitation in his voice.

Once out of the half-lit hallway, Adelman noticed that he had seen medical cadavers with better complexion than the boy. His startlingly red teeth drew his eyes once again to the boy's mouth.

He would be more nervous, but the bar of Xanax melting in his gut didn't leave much room for fear. The mental image of Frank sitting at home, nervously chewing his fingertips like an animal, started to dawn on him.

He was about to tell Frank that he looked good, but that would have only been a half truth. "How are you coming along?" he asked, the doctor script taking over. The way the boy looked at him was nearly sexual in its intensity. So, he didn't wait for a response. "I think that I've come up with another thing we can try." He continued, fumbling for an excuse for the intrusion.

"Oh, I found the solution!" Frank told him still a little timidly, though he was gaining a little more confidence. "The problem though, is I have nothing left. I suck, and I suck, and nothing comes out." Thoughts of what the other boys had done to him drifted in and out of his head, making him feel ill, but he quickly regained what composure he had.

"I need you to get me more blood." He said.

"I work for the free clinic," the doctor explained. "Not even a particularly good one. Hospitals have blood. We can't even afford to get lollipops for kids."

"Oh, ok." Frank said, "Fair enough." He shrugged before he started edging behind the doctor, towards the door. Adelman thought that this was it, the boy was going to ask him to leave. It would be a welcome relief from the butcher shop smell of the apartment. A faint glimmer of the hideous smile returned to the boy's lips.

Throwing the bolt lock with a little *thwunk*, a pang of unease crossed Frank's face when he realized that he was going to have to touch the doctor. From his pocket the boy produced a dull knife smeared in black scabby blood.

His mouth opened, but the voice that came out was completely unlike his own, it sounded more like a boy much younger than he. "Suck the pacifier. Come on baby, suck it!"

Feedlot

In the grant proposal he sent to the Iowa Arts council, he said that he had the desire to explore the death of the American Dream by documenting deterioration of small towns throughout the state. To his surprise, Elijah found a check for two-thousand dollars waiting for him in his mailbox nearly six months later.

Out of dozens he had sent, full of cliché buzzwords about wanting to document this and examine that, they had chosen the one that he had written when he was still half drunk from the night before, nursing a hangover, and had written the outline on a ripped-off cardboard of a case of Budweiser.

It came as a shock, partially because he had forgotten submitting the proposal – among the mountain of others he had sent them in the past few years. Also, because it was one that he had actually still wanted to do. Despite its questionable origins.

They had bought into it! Hurray for mediocrity he had joked to himself. Forty thousand dollars of art school debt finally paying off! He had thought to himself as he stared at the biggest check he had ever seen in his entire career. It wasn't his favorite project, or what he would have thought of as his best idea, but it was at least the first that he could stand behind that others were willing to invest in.

Which kind of made it the best, because an unrealized project is nothing at all.

The ride in was a nightmare, the AC in his truck pissed out a pitiful stream of air that was hardly enough to keep up with the weather. Ninety degrees not counting the humidity. Fuck, with that, it must be nearing one-twenty in how it felt.

The air was warm, wet, stagnant and smelled like the feedlot on the edge of town, that had been replaced by one of those big industrial death factories a dozen miles away. The lot had once supported the town, but when the factory moved in, most of the jobs had become redundant, and so did the lot. The reek of the waste of a million dead pigs filled the air. There had to be miles of shit and viscera rotting away, fermenting away in the humid Iowa air.

The thought of all that feces, death and meat clinched in his belly. Which hadn't even met a glass of milk in the last decade or so. He had let go of his hippy mother's radical politics, but even on his own, he couldn't quite build up the stomach again to eat things that once had a face.

He could really use a drink right now, he thought. His hand shaking a little from the lack of the lubricant that kept him steady. Most of these small towns couldn't even support a gas station anymore, most times the bar was the only business that they *could* sustain. He looked around for one he could order a boilermaker for his lunch, but hadn't had much luck when he had looked for one on Google on the way in.

He fumbled around in his pocket for his flask, but he knew it was dry. He pulled out his pack of Reds and lit up. Most of the money from the council had gone directly to his liver, but what was left over had bought him a decent camera and a subscription to Adobe, along with a few trendy filters he found on Creative Market.

The money you spend making your photos look like they were taken with your cellphone, he had thought, before entering in his PayPal information.

The council had sent him a letter a couple

weeks ago, asking for progress. Other than noting an alarmingly far-right trend in the bathroom graffiti of the bars within walking distance of his apartment, not much.

He was working on a project he *believed* in, but it was still a chore to actually get this going. He had poured over images from the internet to try to find a town, that at least aerially looked like it would be the kind of town that his benefactors were expecting.

Even if it was his vision, he knew that he would have to temper it to their tastes in order to ever see another one of those checks.

He started contemplating another proposal exploring the animosity for undocumented workers among the people of Des Moines but thought maybe he should get going on what he had already been given the funds to do.

Even if it meant actually having to go to these shitty little towns that he had done his best the past decade to avoid, having spent his fair share growing up in one. They're like the feedlots themselves he had thought. You walk in happy and well fed on one side, and the other end is the hammer.

Meth, pregnancy, honey hole jobs that kept you paid just well enough that you don't even question why you're spending fifty hours a week doing a job that would be better suited for a robot than a human being. Enduring alternating shifts.

They had their ways of keeping you in. He shuddered. He had nightmares that he would someday end up in one of those factories even if it wasn't producing dead things. The stale, recycled air, bad coffee, having to ask Hank about his kids every day for all eternity. A hell worse than anything Dante could have dreamed up.

It was all out there waiting for him, he could feel it. He just had to work twice as hard for a fraction of the pay to do his best to avoid it. He flicked the cigarette into the gutter as he stared into the empty storefronts of Main Street.

He was home, or at least a close approximation. All of these towns look exactly the same, a few dozen houses, a town square surrounding a courthouse. A water tower on the edge of town that spelled out its name in big Helvetica bold.

HOPE. It had said as he pulled into town, but from the looks of it, the town had given up much of that. The name had been a nice juicy carrot for the 100 miles he had to travel to it. It would look great on an exhibition catalog. From above, the photos showed that it had nearly everything that he had hoped for.

This town must have once been somebody's Mayberry, but now the general store had "Fuck Walmart" written on the front window with soap. It was good to see that even in these ghost towns, people had kept their midwestern charm!

The idea that he was exploiting the hardship of these people would have been something that bothered him, he thought, if he hadn't come from one of these towns himself. He would probably be right there too, if Becky's mother hadn't made her disappear quicker than Johnny Gosch after she had found out about the consequence of after-prom.

He often wondered if he would be drinking himself blind most nights if Becky was still around, and he still lived in his hometown. It wasn't something that was worth much deliberation. No matter where he would go in the world, the small town would be with him. Even if it was the small town that had rejected him in the first place.

His head baking in the heat; the slow throb of this morning's hangover started creeping back into his temple. He had to get moving, or it would completely take over his concentration. His musette bag with his camera was in the back seat of his shitty little truck that he had bought for a couple hundred dollars, and kept it limping along with whatever snake oil cures he came across in the automotive section of Dollar General.

The truck reeked of urine, after he pissed himself the other night, too drunk to drive home. A cop woke him up in the morning, tapping on his window and telling him it was best time to move on. When the officer had called him "boy" he knew that it was best not to argue the point.

The ring of the officer calling him "boy" had brought back too many memories of why he had left his small town five whole minutes after graduation.

The smell, a small fist that caught him in the stomach and made it churn again; luckily, he didn't have anything in there except for bourbon residue to lose, but was able to keep that as he choked, he grabbed his camera bag and unloaded more Febreze over the interior for the second time today.

He fired off half a dozen shots with a single burst. The anti-corporate sentiment square in the frame. Clicking the review button, he shielded the screen with his other hand and checked to make sure that the automatic exposure was doing the heavy lifting. Thankfully, with technology, even the talentless can pretend they're going to get their pictures into *National Geographic*.

He wasn't talentless, though photography wasn't his focus in school. He was always more of the big idea guy who would fall in love with his own shit easily, but always had a hard time convincing others to march alongside him.

The glare of the sun reflecting off his truck's

rearview mirror scorched his eyes, drawing his attention away from the device. A faint ring of tinnitus filled his ears, due to the lack of sound.

"This town is fucking *dead*," he noted to himself at a hushed volume. "Good." It was the weekend, but he didn't even see kids playing. There were no cars not any evidence that anybody still lived here at all. No obnoxious twit blaring Lynyrd Skynyrd like they were the only person on earth. Nothing.

Not even the ghosts of all those swine were there to bother him. He had wanted a ghost town, and his god Art had provided for him.

He started snapping pictures of the other store fronts, and the potential meth dens across the street whose boarded-up windows were exactly the kind of bullshit he thought the council would eat up. Nothing like placating the audience, he thought to himself as he continued to take wild shots that he didn't even bother checking before moving onto the next subject.

Trust the camera.

He knew that there was something here that he had to capture though. It was this idea that would finally get him the recognition he wanted. Maybe even enough to get some of his other ideas the attention that they deserved. Well that, and more importantly the funding.

Walking and shooting, he fumbled another cigarette out of his pocket with his free hand and lit it with a practiced one-handed grace that could get him laid if he were at the bar. The smoke made him remember that he had lungs. Something he often forgot. The cloud gathered around him, as there was no wind to carry it away. Turning his head back, he could see the trail of smoke behind him like breadcrumbs that might lead him back to his truck.

He snapped a picture. There might be a metaphor there, that he could figure out the justification for later. He didn't believe in god, but he did believe in capital "A" Art. Art you could justify, even if you only believed in an individual piece just a little bit.

The last time he had ever gotten any money for his "art," he had gone around similar towns and had interviewed so-called "abductees". He would sit there with his iPhone and record them recount how squeaky clean little gray people would tell them all about how the world was coming to an end soon, if we don't stop using straws, or whatever.

In the six months that he had done so, he had never met one that didn't have the craziest fucking look on their face when they told their story.

At the show, people laughed and shook their heads.

He wasn't so sure, though, whether they were crazy or lying. "Maybe the mothership came down and took this entire fucking town." Elijah laughed to himself quietly and took another puff. A half-scavenged bird lay on the sidewalk. He stopped and took its picture. "Except for you, little birdie, and whatever fed on your itty-bitty insides."

The focus fixed on a maggot coming out of its eye, the money shot he was after.

"Why the fuck am I talking to a dead bird?" he asked himself. "And why the fuck am I talking to myself? This quiet must be getting to me." His eyes were drawn off the bird, to a familiar sight. "B-A-R, well I'll be damned. Talk to you later, bird," he said, before making his way to the window. Through the tint, he could see that the lights were on.

No music, but the they *looked* open. It might be his lucky day after all. The door came open, but with some effort, the pressure of the air outside sealing the door tightly. The inside was empty, the bartender must be out back having a cigarette, he thought. It's a damn shame that not even the owner of bars can smoke in their own establishments these days.

The building was small, with a stage bigger than the area the audience could watch from. No tables, but a row of stools stood in front of the bar; a bottle of Jack Daniels stood center-court on its top with an empty glass next to it. Don't mind if I do, I guess I'll just pay him when he comes back. Pouring himself a healthy quantity, he sat down and lifted the glass straight back.

And then he poured another, before swinging around and taking in the room, his camera hand shooting wildly. He often relied on the stabilizer a little too heavily, even if the pictures came out blurry he could always blame it on artistic intent. Clicking preview, the first picture that popped up on the screen was of the stage. "That's weird," he said to himself, downing the drink.

Standing up, he walked over to the stage and on the back wall he saw a pig's skull; with a big step he got up to look at it better. Firing off a couple shots, he looked closer. Between its eyes, a perfect little bullet hole. From the size of it, when it was alive, it must have weighed more than his truck. "Jesus," Elijah said, to nobody in particular.

On the floor below the skull were fresh flowers, and the type of candles that he had always associated with the times that his mother had made go with his grandmother to mass. Beads and icons of saints filled out the strange altar.

The word Santeria popped into his head, but it was much too Wonder Bread for that.

"Who the fuck worships at a bar? Who the fuck worships Miss Piggy?" he said, just loud enough to hear himself talk.

"Alright *boy*, time best for ya to git goin'." A drawl that he recognized too distinctly from his childhood called out from behind him. It was a voice that would be attached to a trucker hat that said Life's Too Short to Dance with Ugly Women, and Reeltree camouflage.

Turning around, he was surprised to see that the man was dressed in a priest's cassock. Behind him two men in t-shirts and blue jeans. Maybe I rushed to judgment a little there, he thought. Though the Neoprene half-masks with a print of the lower half of a pig skull they wore put him ill at ease.

"You don't belong here, *boy*." The priest continued, pointing to the bar's door.

"Alright, I didn't mean anything by it. I'm just here on an art project. You know, photographs?" He pointed at his camera as he stepped down from the stage, holding his free hand up to show that he meant no harm.

"Get going," the priest demanded, nodding his head towards the door.

As he passed the men, the smell of body odor was so thick that it smelled liked chili. Elijah's stomach pulled tight around the whiskey it contained. They didn't move at him, so he kept walking.

The sunshine outside was so bright, it nearly

blinded him. In the street were a dozen men, fit and tense. Wearing the same masks as the men inside. They stood silently, staring at Elijah as he struggled to focus.

A small murmur spread throughout the men, before erupting in scattered calls of "He's here to take a job!" they cried out in a blaze that was hotter than the pavement.

"We have nothing for you!" one yelled, as a stone came hurtling out of his hand, hitting Elijah in the nose, breaking it with a snap that he could feel through his entire body. "Go back to where you came from!" he continued, spitting at the ground.

The men closed in around him, their hands roughly shoving him every which way. He could feel their hands like claws ripping at him, punching him, pushing him to the ground. Their boots came down hard on the outsider's body.

The last thing that he saw was the waffle of a boot coming down straight for his eye.

His head was throbbing, he couldn't see anything, but he could hear the men around him.

Had they blinded him?

The room went silent moments before the priest addressed the crowd.

"We live in troubled times," he began. "And like most troubled times, the threat doesn't come from within. It's always an outsider who brings it. Sometimes, we have to do what must be done in order to keep the purity and sanctity of the community alive."

Elijah could feel something hard tap at his chest.

"Even if we do not take great pleasure in it."

The hood that covered Elijah's face was then lifted, and he could see the men around him, their faces grotesque with anger and fear.

"Even if he doesn't work for the *goliath* that has ruined us. We cannot let him bring word to the outside." The priest concluded.

The crowd started chanting, low at first, gradually becoming suffocating in their volume. "Feed the pig! Feed the Pig! Feed the Pig!" From the edge of the stage, a hog, bigger than any that Elijah ever saw in his life, was being led to him. Its milky white eyes were blind, completely unaware of its surroundings.

He remembered seeing a picture from his grandmother's bible. Moses coming down from the mountain and those ancient Jews, scared and not knowing what to do next, worshiping at the feet of a bull.

The priest's hand wiped away the blood from the outsider's broken nose and put the hand up to the pig's snout. Its tongue lapped up it happily. The priest pet the animal's head, leaving a print of blood and saliva between its dead eyes. The smell of shit that came off its nearly albino skin was overpowering.

Leading it to more, the priest guided the pig, which began licking Elijah's face before taking its initial bite. What was it that his grandmother had said? *Don't trust those folks in small towns, they don't know god from Sunday dinner.*

Small towns will never let you go.

The Butterfly of Ugly

Thwack.

Up here — with no one around, I feel like a ghost.

Though, even when I was on stage with all the vampires and crawlers staring at me, I would get the feeling that I wasn't there.

The smells of the woods and the aching of my muscles are the only things that betray that I'm still here.

Or are they a figment of my imagination?

Can the dead feel imaginary pain, so they can hold onto their humanity?

I can't even remember the last time I was in a room with someone else who acknowledged my existence.

The smell of skin. The taste of cherry Chapstick on ragged lips. Our clothes scattered around the bedroom floor of the trailer. The sweet voice of M whispering in the darkness. As we lay naked and vulnerable to each other and the chill that filled the room like a cold, cruel god bearing down on us.

Thwack.

Another log split into two; I toss the pieces aside and place the next on the block. I feel like I've been doing forever, and that I will be doing this still when Jesus decides it's time to pull the plug.

Ol' Sissyfists got nothing on me.

The woods are full of watchers. I don't know who they are or what they want. If they want anything from me at all. I've even felt them inside my cabin.

They're in there, too. I feel their wondrous eyes on me, watching and waiting.

Sometimes I ask myself which of my many monsters they are, though when it comes down to it... Does it matter?

Thwack.

Suddenly, the skies are full of Monarchs as they flutter and fly their way back to where their grandfathers had left last spring. I can hear their wings working against the wind. Their heads full of their father's memories.

Like when I was *my* dad, the jungles were thick and the ears I wore around my neck were greeted with free beer and congratulations.

When I was eight, my mom would take me to a little building in the woods. It was odd that such a big glass and concrete structure would be out there in the heart of nature. Like a middle finger to god.

Not like the cracking logs walls of my haven out here in this wilderness.

In that monstrosity, the doctors in white

would take me and a bunch of other children into a room. *The sound of butterfly wings was deafening.* We couldn't walk anywhere without stepping on a few.

I felt so bad, but they told me to stop crying and not to worry. There would be more where they came from. They wouldn't live through the week, anyway.

Nothing persists in this world, especially anything beautiful.

M's brown hair just touched her shoulder, I would brush it back and kiss the porcelain skin of her neck.

When the band played, I tried to make my guitar sound like the wings of those butterflies, deafening but soft, as easy to kill as gingerly stepping down.

Nobody believed me when I told them what happened. They just thought that ol' Jack was off the medicine again. Take him back to the old woods with the doctors who study him like an insect under glass.

Or like the last child left in a room. Covered in blood and the struggling bodies of butterflies that never saw the outside of those sterile walls.

Before they shoved me into the machine that took pictures of the inside of my head.

Without M, what was the point of beauty anyway? I broke up the band and came out here "to get away". Though, now I realize that there's no getting away.

Thwack.

At least I had gotten away from the vampires, I tell myself. The leeches who were always wanting just a little bit more than I was able to give them. It wasn't their fault they wanted so much, or that I had so little to give.

M would tell me about how much I had to give and that I was her knight in flannel armor, she thought that was funny. With her dad gone, I don't know what I was protecting her from. His necklace of ears, the bruises on her body that I would attempt to kiss away.

Maybe it was from something she saw staring into the deep puddles, where she said she could see the future. But did she see what would happen to her? Would she have been able to see my past if I asked? To tell me what happened when they had closed those doors? What they had locked up tight inside my memory.

Thwack.

The woods are strange and full of truths that we try to escape from in cities. The sprawl that I would watch from the inside our tour van driving through god-knows-where that was equally as empty and unpromising as the last.

So here I am in the woods again, but without the doctors, without the vampires. Without the other children, who would start to cannibalize each other in that room.

Gnashing teeth, the whimpers of the weak. I, somehow, was the only one left.

Thwack.

The doctors would give us the Jesus crackers and tell us to wait. The images that would fill my head were like nothing I could ever put into words, no matter how many songs I would sing.

What I saw was more beautiful than any melody and worse than M's body, still and mutilated like a butterfly crushed into the carpet. Her blood like fresh pennies on the air. I flashed back the room with the children, or did I flash forward to our trailer?

My hair was matted with their blood, or was it hers?

All I knew was that my vampires had found her and had extinguished the light that kept me swimming; after what they had done, I began to drown.

My band-mates would pretend they had never known M, even when I showed them pictures. They were just worried that the band breaking up would send them back to delivering pizzas and writing zines.

Thwack.

Sometimes I wonder if I could go back up on that stage, knowing it was them that had crushed my butterfly. I wonder if they would pull my wings off, too. Or maybe the doctors put just enough ugly in me to keep me alive?

Nothing beautiful persists.

Thwack.

Every time I opened my door, I knew that I'd see her there. Her ragged red wings pooled under her, ready to carry her away to the other side.

The pile of wood is deep, not nearly as high as the cabin had once been. I don't know where I'll go once it gets dark. Around me are the other children, unaged by the last 20 years, and still sticky with gore.

Their bodies covered in the maddening patterns of those bugs they had crushed in their exit from this world.

ALSO FROM FILTHY LOOT

F•CKED UP STORIES 1, 2 & 3

LAZERMALL

DOG DOORS TO OUTER SPACE

THE GOD IN THE HILLS
Jon Steffens

THE VINES THAT ATE THE STARLET
Madeleine Swann

PARTICIPATION TROPHY
Ira Rat

TEENAGE GRAVE

FILTHYLOOT.COM

www.ingramcontent.com/pod-product-compliance
Lightning Source LLC
LaVergne TN
LVHW092056060526
838201LV00047B/1420